# HUMAN TOWN

## ALAN DURANT
## ANNA DOHERTY

D0335495

ACC. No: 07096343

TINY OWL

*For Bella and Sue with love Alsie*

*For some of my favourite humans:*
*Jordan, Keira and Lotte – Anna*

Copyright © Tiny Owl Publishing 2022
Text © Alan Durant 2022
Illustrations © Anna Doherty  2022

Alan Durant has asserted her right under the Copyright, Designs
and Patents Act 1988 to be identified as Author of this work.
Anna Doherty has asserted her right under the Copyright, Designs
and Patents Act 1988 to be identified as Illustrator of this work.

First published in the UK in 2022
by Tiny Owl Publishing, London

For teacher resources and more information,
visit www.tinyowl.co.uk
#HumanTownTO

All rights reserved. No part of this publication may be reproduced, stored in a retrieval
system, or transmitted in any form or by any means, electronic, mechanical, photocopying,
recording, or otherwise, without the prior permission of the publisher, nor be otherwise
circulated in any form of binding or cover other than that in which it is published and
without a similar condition being imposed on the subsequent purchaser.

A catalogue record for this book is available from the British Library.
ISBN 9781910328835

Printed in China

# HUMAN TOWN

## ALAN DURANT
## ANNA DOHERTY

It was a hot, sunny day.

Junior and his family were by the river.

Junior and his sister Lulu were splashing each other with water to stay cool.

"Can we go to Human Town? Please, Mum!" Junior cried.

"Please, Mumma," Lulu echoed.

"I suppose so," said Mum. "But I think you might find it boring. There aren't many humans left, you see."

HUMAN TOWN

ALL WELCOME!
TICKETS AVAILABLE
AT THE GATE

"Human Town is cool!" said Junior.

So Mum and Dad, Junior and Lulu went to Human Town.
A rhino was on guard at the gate.
He nodded to the rules.

# Rules

1. You must not touch or feed the humans.
2. You must keep to the paths at all times.
3. You must not trample buildings or other structures.
4. No loud noises.
5. No souvenirs.

THE HUNTING AND EATING OF HUMAN BEINGS
IN THIS PARK IS STRICTLY PROHIBITED.

"We're vegetarians," said Dad.

"Me too," said the rhino.
"But you can't trust the lions and the other big cats."

The elephant family plodded into Human Town.

"Now, humans can be dangerous and unpredictable, so don't get too close," Dad warned.

Lulu cuddled up to Mum.

"Come on!" Junior shouted.

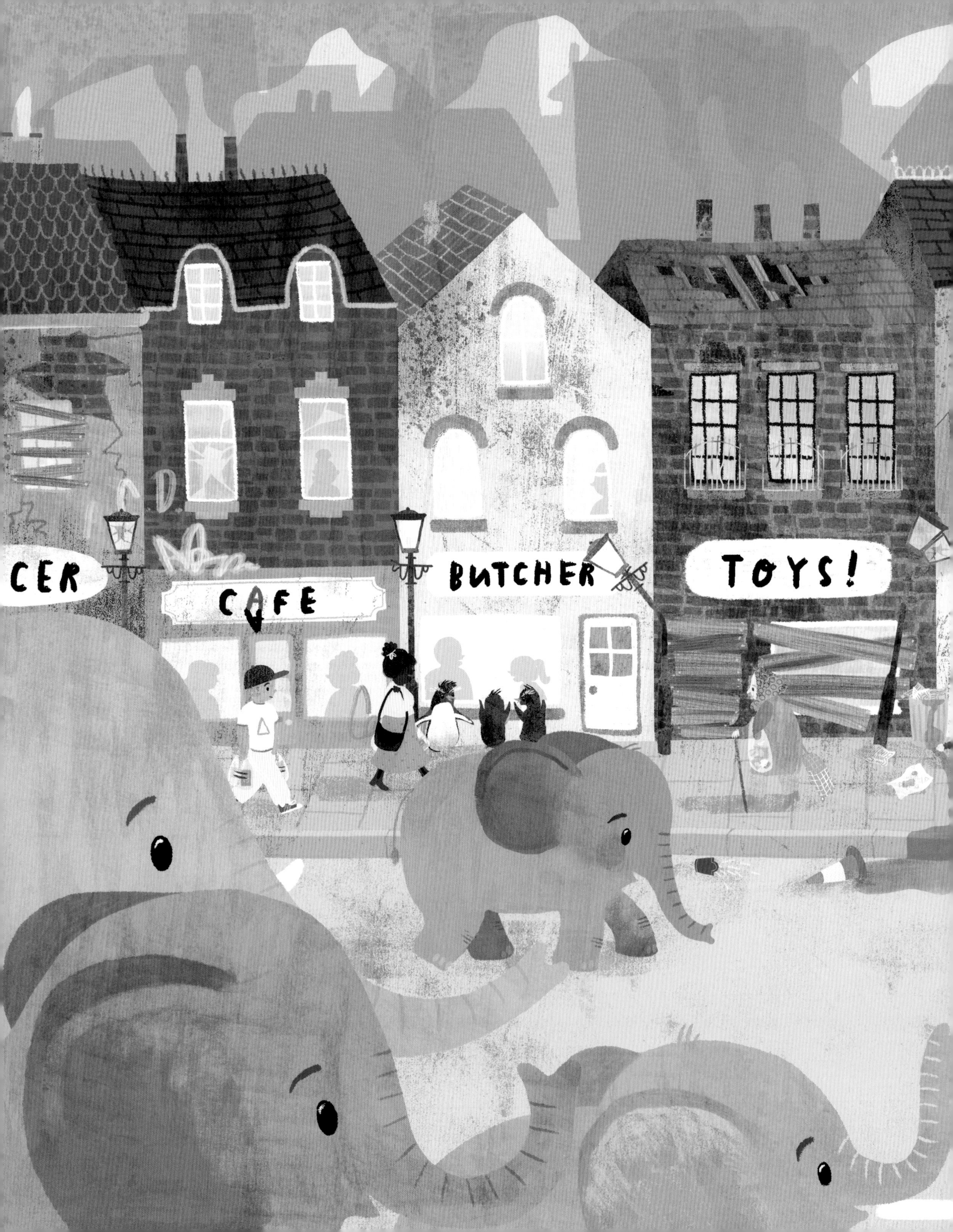
CER
CAFE
BUTCHER
TOYS!

First they came to MAIN STREET.
"These buildings are called shops," said Dad.

They watched humans going in with nothing
and coming out carrying bulging bags.

"What a lot of things," said Junior.
"Humans love things," said Mum.
"Things make them happy," Dad added.

The biggest shop of all was called SUPERMARKET.

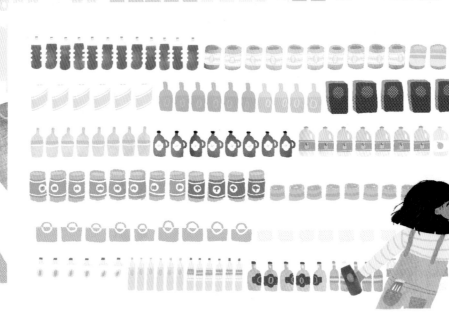

CEREAL & SNACKS →

FRUIT & VEG →

"This is where humans get their food," said Dad.

"Look, bananas!" cried Lulu.
"Humans do eat fruit," said Mum. "But they also like to eat cows and sheep and chickens."

"Chickens! Yuck!" yelled Junior. "That's disgusting."

"You can't judge them like us," said Dad.
"They're wild animals."

They walked down some more streets.
Then they came to the PARK.

"They're playing football,"
said Dad. He sighed.

"When I was young there were a lot
more humans. We used to come and
watch them play games. It was funny
and exciting – especially when they
scored a goal."

"Now, it's just sad and boring,"
said Junior disappointedly.

"You can say that again," said a giraffe,
whose family was also watching.

They walked on past a stream that was full of rubbish.

"It smells nasty here," Lulu complained.

"And the air is hard to breathe," said Junior.

"That's one of the reasons humans are dying out," said Mum.

"They don't look after their environment."

At that moment, something passed by noisily with smoke coming out of its bottom.

"A farting car!"
Junior exclaimed.

Dad had told him
about farting cars.

"Language,
Junior,"
Mum said.

They went to a CHURCH ... and a CINEMA ... and a SCHOOL.

But there were no humans there.

"When I was young, these places were full of humans," sighed Mum.

"We used to love watching the boys and girls doing their lessons. They were so cute."

The humans they saw
outside the HOUSES
weren't cute.

STOLEN

"That's another reason why there aren't many humans left," said Dad. "They're always fighting each other."

The elephants peered
into the houses.

There were lots and lots
of things.

There was a human lying
down watching a box
with pictures.

"What's that?"
asked Junior.

"It's called Teevee," Dad explained.

"Humans love Teevee," said Mum.

"Look, elephants!" cried Lulu, pointing at the box.

"Boring," said Junior.

PICNIC
AREA

The elephant family had a picnic.
Then, it was time to go home.

"I did warn you that it might not be very interesting," said Mum to the children that evening at bedtime.

"Mum, Dad said that humans will soon be extinct. Is that true?" asked Junior.

"I'm afraid so – especially if those big cats keep poaching them," Mum sighed with a shake of her big head.

"That's awful," said Junior sadly.
"Imagine a world with no humans ..."

He thought for a moment.
"I hope that never happens to us."